For Carole and her family.
Best wishes,
Lola Sneyd.

Classy
Cats

Other Books by Lola Sneyd
Illustrated by Doug Sneyd

Nature's Big Top (Simon & Pierre, 1987)

The Concrete Giraffe (Simon & Pierre, 1984)

The Asphalt Octopus (Simon & Pierre, 1982)

Classy Cats

Lola Sneyd

poetry by Lola Sneyd

illustrated by Doug Sneyd

Simon & Pierre
Toronto, Canada

We would like to express our gratitude to the Canada Council and the Ontario Arts Council for their support.

Marian M. Wilson, Publisher

Copyright © 1991 by Lola Sneyd. All rights reserved.

Cover and design copyright © 1991 by Simon & Pierre Publishing Co. Ltd. /
Les Éditions Simon & Pierre Ltée. All rights reserved.

No part of this book may be reproduced or transmitted in any form or by any means, electronic or mechanical, including photocopying and recording, information storage and retrieval systems, without permission in writing from the publisher, except by a reviewer who may quote brief passages in a review. Permissions starting on the acknowledgments page are a continuation of the copyright page.

ISBN 0-88924-209-7

2 3 4 5 • 6 5 4 3 2   Second Printing 2001

Canadian Cataloguing in Publication Data

Sneyd, Lola
    Classy cats

Poems.
ISBN 0-88924-209-7

1. Cats - Juvenile poetry.   I. Sneyd, Doug.
II. Title.

PS8587.N48C5 1991   j811'.54   C91-094062-2
PZ8.3.S54C1 1991

Cover Illustration: Doug Sneyd
Design: C. P. Wilson

Editor: Marian M. Wilson
Associate Editor: Jean Paton
Typesetting: Peter Goodchild

Printed and Bound in Canada

Order from
Simon & Pierre Publishing Company Limited /
Les Éditions Simon & Pierre Ltée.
P.O. Box 280 Adelaide Street Postal Station
Toronto, Ontario, Canada M5C 2J4

For Marian Wilson,
who suggested this book
in fond memory of

Simon (Blue Russian) and Pierre (Siamese)
the two literary cats since 1972

and Sylvestre (Abyssinian)
the official greeter of the publishing house
for many years

Contents

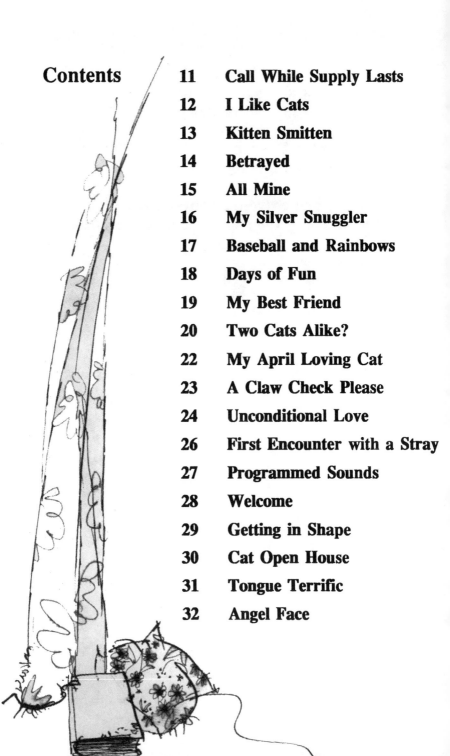

- 11   Call While Supply Lasts
- 12   I Like Cats
- 13   Kitten Smitten
- 14   Betrayed
- 15   All Mine
- 16   My Silver Snuggler
- 17   Baseball and Rainbows
- 18   Days of Fun
- 19   My Best Friend
- 20   Two Cats Alike?
- 22   My April Loving Cat
- 23   A Claw Check Please
- 24   Unconditional Love
- 26   First Encounter with a Stray
- 27   Programmed Sounds
- 28   Welcome
- 29   Getting in Shape
- 30   Cat Open House
- 31   Tongue Terrific
- 32   Angel Face

33	My Sweet Kitten
34	Cat Heaven
35	Big Game Hunter
36	Watch Cat
37	Cat Proud
38	Security Guard
39	Last Warning
40	Thanks, But No Thanks
41	Scat, Cat!
42	Space Contact?
43	I Talk to My Plants
44	Let's Be Friends
45	Repeat Performance
46	Cat-Nap
47	A Home Run
48	My Olympic Tabby Cat
49	Independence
50	Photo Finish
51	My Educated Cat
52	Purrr Ppplease
53	Cat Shadow Art in Winter's Snow
54	Fluffy
55	Three Times You're Out!

56	City Survivor
57	My Eskimo Cat
58	Friendship
59	A Musical Tale
60	Frustration
61	Along a Country Road
62	My Anchor
63	Cat Class Act
64	My Singular Cat
65	My Gift
66	Nap-Mates
67	Magnetic Attraction
69	Acknowledgements
70	About the author, Lola Sneyd
	About the illustrator, Doug Sneyd

CALL WHILE
SUPPLY LASTS

Cute cuddly kittens—for free
Have a built-in love guarantee . . .
Motors are permanently wired
And batteries are never required.

I LIKE CATS

I like cats
because of this known feature . . .
Each cat is
A complicated creature.

KITTEN SMITTEN

Today
I'm smitten
with a calico cat
and her
tie-dyed kitten.

**BETRAYED
(MOVING DAY)**

**Unblinking amber eyes
sadly searching for a solution**

**Yesterday beloved
free to roam**

**Today deserted
caged in this carrier**

How can you do this to me?

ALL MINE

Crooked tail
broken teeth
gravelly purr
variegated patchy fur

dignified king of the back yard

so special

my very own
motor-mouth
cat

MY SILVER SNUGGLER

My tiny baby kitten
Is soft and silvery grey,
She's my favourite playmate
Who plays with me all day.

I tell her all my secrets . . .
She never squeals on me,
And when I try to hug her
Her whiskers tickle me.

She bats around my toys and games,
She messes up my room,
And when I try to sweep it up
She plays tag with my broom.

She has her wicker basket
To rest her weary head,
But I wake up with her snuggling
Beside me on the bed.

Good Morning, Baby Kitten!

BASEBALL AND RAINBOWS

For hours you sit
by the slowly dripping
tap in the sink
Your golden paw
bats water drop home runs

The morning sun
spotlights rainbows
on your glistening whiskers

DAYS OF FUN

My neighbour said, "Life's boring,
Same dull things to be done."
But since she got a kitten
Her days are full of fun.

MY BEST FRIEND

My cat runs to meet me,
Cheers me at day's end . . .
Because she can't talk
She's my favourite friend.

TWO CATS ALIKE?

Hypnotised
you stare at
that other Siamese
usurper
of your domain

only the whirr
of the can-opener
entices you to leave
your kingdom

on silent pads
you return
stretch your elastic neck
to breaking
and peer around
the corner

she's still there
peeking around the
mirror's bevelled edge
trying to
outstare you

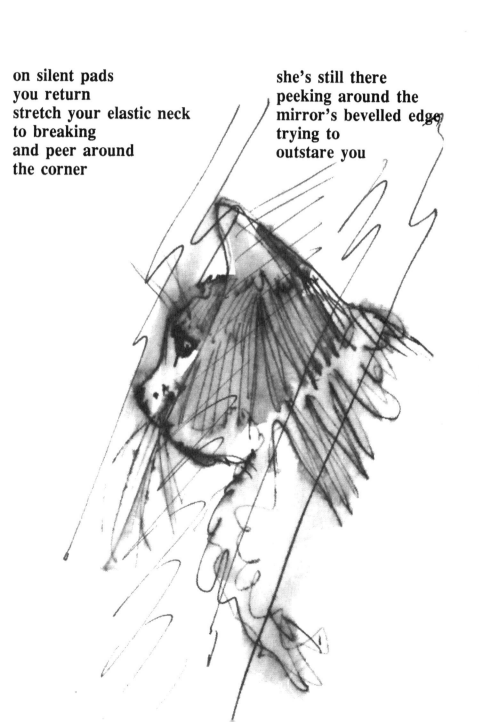

MY APRIL LOVING CAT

I know where you've been . . .
My pants and my shoes
Show your adventurous
Stroll-in-the-mud clues.

My nose tells me that
you're April rain fresh,
My clothes say you lack
The paws that refresh.

A CLAW CHECK PLEASE

Before you lavish
your affection on me
Please hide your claws
inside your toe pockets
Instead of me

UNCONDITIONAL LOVE

Unconditional love
is
a kitten

All it asks for is
to be petted
and played with,
      cat food and water,
      a collar and leash,
      cat toys for playtime,
      a tall scratching post.

Soon you will have
a cuddly homebody
who will always trust you
or
a "Don't-touch-my-fur"
independent cat,
who'll add mystery and intrigue
as it shares your home.

Your cat's language of feeling
will speak louder than words.

FIRST ENCOUNTER WITH A STRAY

I offer you
> dry cat food
> moist cat food
> saucers of milk
> cut up chicken breasts
> bits of sauteed liver
> smoked salmon on
> kitty crackers

You narrow your dark eyes at me
Haughtily you turn away

I ignore you

You leap onto the table
and gobble up
dinner table scraps

how was I to know you were
a table scrap lover
alley-cat?

PROGRAMMED SOUNDS

To a hungry cat
Food is a warm hug,
And a can-opener is
a cat ALERT bug.

WELCOME

Tarzan jungles in
hanging flower pots
Polished brass cats and
wooden candlesticks
Little brown jugs with
tan cork plugs
Tall crystal vases and
old pickle crocks
Stained glass artwork
twirling in the draft
Worn pink sheet fluttering
neighbours moving in

In a shiny blue china
flowered chamber pot
a trailing philodendron
touches my kitten's happy face
that smiles down at me

GETTING IN SHAPE

Around and around
you chase your tail
then play catch
with a make-believe cat

leap at the wall
to catch a fly
then chase and box
an invisible foe
and catch it between
your swift forepaws

are you practicing to be
a baseball catcher
or a live fly-swatter

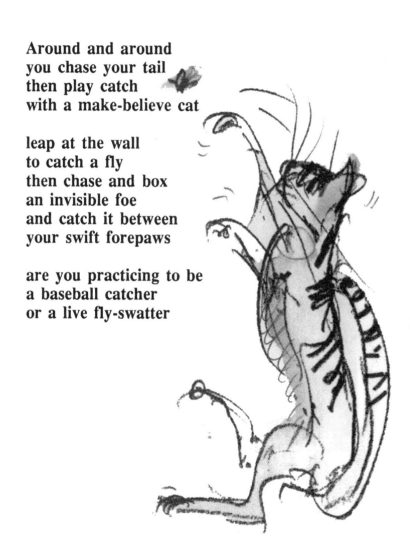

CAT OPEN HOUSE

You ignore my friendship . . .
Then tell me why, please,
you prefer playing host to
a family of fleas?

TONGUE TERRIFIC

Rows of fleshy spikes unseen
With tiny crevices in between

Act as spoon and also cup,
Milk and water they soon lap up.

After meals they wash fur clean,
Scrub and comb, brush and preen.

I lose my brush and I lose my comb.
Lucky kitten is born with her own.

ANGEL FACE

You curl yourself around
the dark green cedar's
rough grey-brown trunk
expertly climb
the inner
circular staircase

your fluffy tail hugs
the home base trunk

the cedar sways gently

at the top
you turn
twitch your white whiskers
and grin down at me

king of the castle

an orange tree-top
Christmas angel
in July

MY SWEET KITTEN

You've climbed the curtains
And scratched the chair,
You've snagged the towels
And pawed my hair,

You've tangled my wool,
Shed hair on my pants,
Played ball with the cushions,
Uprooted my plants.

You've chewed book covers,
And purr innocently.
Your cute kitten capers
Will never fool me.

You're not a sweet kitten,
You're a cat-astrophe!

CAT HEAVEN

Sound asleep
you wake with a start
eagerly rush to welcome
it

ecstatically
you snuggle up
lean into it
rub your back
     your head
     your tail
     against it
roll over on your back
your plump black belly
invites its gentle caress
you stretch
purring with pleasure

a voyeur
I watch
your intimate love affair
with my hand vacuum

BIG GAME HUNTER

Fierce as a tiger
Swift as a flea
Silently you zig
zag through my garden
tracking
stalking
a fat ferocious rat?
a vicious grey field mouse?
an armoured ebony cricket?
a giant fighting frog?

no
you're after swifter
more elusive game
and proudly drop it at my feet
summer's first flitting
white butterfly

WATCH CAT

A leisurely evening stroll
up one side of the street
and down the other

a kitty cookie
midnight snack

I hear your
all's-right-with-the-world signal
as you purr yourself to sleep
on the foot of my bed

Now I can sleep

CAT PROUD

He says with pride,
    My cat can talk
    and hold a conversation.
I know it's true . . .
    On moonlit nights
    he wakes up half the nation.

SECURITY GUARD

Hour after hour
morning after morning
you patrol
my sunny front porch
telling the robins
starlings, sparrows
pigeons and squirrels:
"PRIVATE PROPERTY
Trespassers will be prosecuted"

LAST WARNING

Leave my plants alone

One more dig and
I'll shoot

I'll score

My trusty gun
never lets me down

(as long as I remember
to load it
with water ammunition)

THANKS, BUT NO THANKS

Proudly you donate
a plump field mouse
to the family food supply

an act of love?
of gratitude?

sharing or
just showing off?

SCAT, CAT!

Scat, Cat!
Can't you see that
I'm trying to type?

Scat, Cat!
Quit playing bat
With the keys as I type.

Now see what you've done—

You've spilled the waste basket
all over the floor,
and batted some pages
right out of the door.

I guess that I'll not
get anything done,
because you insist
it's time to have fun.

Come, chase this balled paper
then sit at my feet.
My cat-break is over
I've a deadline to keep.

SPACE CONTACT?

Amidst the perpetual
traffic sounds
coming in the window
and the stereo's blaring noise
How do you hear a sound
that freaks you out
and makes you jump
like a jack-in-the-box?

You freak me out

And I still
can't hear a thing

I TALK TO MY PLANTS

Poor tiny plants,
so droopy and sad
cheer up,
I'll place you on this window sill
now you can turn
to greet the sun
and smile.

CRASH!

                CRASH!

                              CRASH!

there goes another one

Poor tiny plants.

Jealous cat!

LET'S BE FRIENDS

I turned the sprinkler on
Before I took a look
To see if you had found
A secret cat-nap nook.

I said "I'm sorry" quickly,
And didn't laugh at you.
I lavish treats and hugs,
Cheer you when you're blue.

You know I've always been
The best friend that you've had.
You barely tolerate me . . .
Your cat grudge makes me sad.

Come, let's be friends again,
And I'll remember that
You own my yard, and that you are
A water-hater cat.

REPEAT PERFORMANCE

Silently
cautiously
you climb
the paper white birch tree
stalking
that fledgling sparrow

it flies

you leap
and drop to the ground

again and again

and you still believe
you can fly

are you sure you
haven't used up
your other nine lives?

CAT-NAP

In the shade of the old lilac bush
she sniffs and turns around
with a flick of her paws
sends a twig flying
in time to cat music
relaxes her cat muscles
one by one
inside her sleek shiny black fur
tucks in her front paws
back paws
her white-tipped tail
bows her head
chin resting on tail tip
a siesta-shaped ball
she dreams cat dreams

A HOME RUN

I call and call
When you finally come
you slide into
your feeding dish
like a batter
sliding into home base

MY OLYMPIC TABBY CAT

Dancing leaves invite you
Lightly you bounce
down the wooden steps
Paw bat
the wind-tossed
golden birch and bronze oak leaves
Race around the old oak tree
Faster   faster
The leaves dance higher
You leap and dance
Higher   higher

A dry oak leaf catches
against the wooden fence

You pounce

Proudly you carry
your bronze medal to me

And race
to capture
the gold

INDEPENDENCE

Dance cat dance
by the light of the moon
prowl the backyards
patrol the fence
be chief inspector
of all you survey
till morning light
then rest
when humans take charge
of everything else

but never of you

PHOTO FINISH

A cat
  chasing its shadow down the street.
   Neat!

MY EDUCATED CAT

You arch your silver furry back
into an upside down U

Blink your O eyes

Wiggle your triangle nose

Open your upside-down mouth

Swish your long l tail

Raise it and
turn it into
a fluffy question mark

I'd answer you
but I haven't learned cat language

PURRRR PPPPLEASE

My ears are nipped
My nose is froze
My whiskers frosted
I've ice for toes

Fleas lose their flea-hold
On shivery me
So please take me home
I'm flea-free and FREE

CAT SHADOW ART IN WINTER'S SNOW

They zig when you zig
zag when you zag
race when you race
pounce when you pounce
halt when you halt

preliminary sketches
cat silhouette
creations in nature's studio

nightly viewing
at the
Moonlight Snow Galleries

FLUFFY

Quietly daydreaming
he sits by the fireplace

The children chant
"Here, Kitty, Kitty."

He raises his white plumed tail
stalks majestically
across the room
inserts himself
beneath the sofa

On hands and knees they plead,
"Here, Kitty, Kitty,
Come, sweet Fluffy,
Come and play."

Tiny probing fingers are
rewarded with a hiss
                    a bite

Respect me,
I'm a cat,
and no cat wants to play
dress up!

THREE TIMES YOU'RE OUT!

Tiny golden kitten
trapped in our tall oak tree
meowing frantically.

I climb the tallest ladder
and reach for you.

You climb higher
and like a high wire actor
quickly prance along
that bouncing way-out branch
cling precariously,
meow panic-ly.

The cat-loving fireman
in the red cherry-picker
rescues you
twice in one week.

You repeat your spotlight act.

I call.
He says: No way, lady!
I plead.
He says: hunger pangs
will force him down,
besides
I've never yet seen a cat skeleton
in a tree.

CITY SURVIVOR

On winter's cold pavement
you sit at attention
silver bushy tail blanket
draped gracefully over
your frozen cat feet
tucked around your
freezing haunches
green eyes on the alert
pleading for
a shop door to open

MY ESKIMO CAT

You sit on my knees and purr
I stroke your thick white fur
You snuggle closer
then duck my kisses

Independent or just
avoiding my germs?

Fleetingly
you place your nose
next to mine

A quick rub
that's all

When did you visit
the land of ice and snow?

FRIENDSHIP

If I could bottle
    your strength
    your courage
    your contented independence
I'd create a formula and
become a millionaire

Since I can't

Your way of life
is rubbing off on me

I'm learning to relax
and find happiness
in having you
for my friend

A MUSICAL TALE

Your silky smooth
black baton tail
directs an invisible
feline orchestra.

Your body gently sways
to a mystical melody,

your magic spell
captures me.

My movements mirror yours,
as side by side we dance
around the ballroom floor,

the morning sun spotlights us:
paints moving silhouettes
on the kitchen wall.

FRUSTRATION

I give you love
food and attention—
You keep me at a distance,
and won't come when I call.

My neighbour ignores you—
You shower her with attention,
beg to be petted,
and purr kitten love songs
to her.

How can *I* get
on your
love wave-length?

ALONG A COUNTRY ROAD

Thin vertical slits
of glowing green lights
penetrate the darkness
twin clues
that a cat is on the prowl . . .
That I'm not alone.

MY ANCHOR

You are
my link with nature,
with sanity.

You are
my oasis,
my refuge from
the outside,
the technological world.

You are
my anchor with reality.

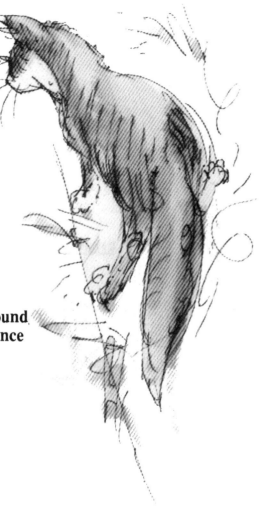

CAT CLASS ACT

Black belly to the ground
you slink along the fence
intent on
that early morning
worm-pulling robin

fluid-like
you climb the fence

a twig falls

you pounce
sideswipe the redwood picnic table
flip sidewards to the dew-silvered grass

sheepishly you look around

regain your dignity
tail held banner high
you walk away

MY SINGULAR CAT

I pamper and praise you,
keep your days free from strife . . .
But still you ignore me
And lead your own life.

MY GIFT

Treasure seeking
you stroll across
the dew sprinkled lawn
investigate the fragrant
     cedar hedge
tread cautiously around
     the thorny rose bushes
sniff the white
     lily of the valley bells
and the air's cool dampness

adventure over
you return

quivering darts of light
radiate from
your gift to me
a dew-drop diamond
on the tip of your nose

NAP-MATES

Exhausted
they sleep entwined
his tail curled around
her tiny arm
her wee fist
tucked between
his front paws
weary, worn out playmates
all day long

she
his crawling cat
he
her calico kitten mouse

MAGNETIC ATTRACTION

Get one kitten
feed it
love it

and it will grow up
and bring you
cats
and cats
and more cats